The World's LONGEST SOCK

Written and Illustrated by
Juliann Law

WORTHY
kids ™

ISBN: 978-1-5460-0258-1

WorthyKids
Hachette Book Group
1290 Avenue of the Americas
New York, NY 10104

Library of Congress Cataloging-in-Publication Data

Names: Law, Juliann, author, illustrator.
Title: The world's longest sock / written and illustrated by Juliann Law.
Description: New York, NY : WorthyKids, [2022] | Audience: Ages 4–7. |
   Summary: "In order to break a world record, a fierce knitting
   competition spans the globe but a message of cooperation knits the world
   together"— Provided by publisher.
Identifiers: LCCN 2021057692 | ISBN 9781546002581 (hardcover)
Subjects: CYAC: Competition (Psychology)—Fiction. | Knitting—Fiction. |
   World records—Fiction. | LCGFT: Picture books.
Classification: LCC PZ7.1.L38255 Wo 2022 | DDC [E]—dc23
LC record available at https://lccn.loc.gov/2021057692

Designed by Eve DeGrie

Printed and bound in China
APS
10 9 8 7 6 5 4 3 2 1

World's Biggest
Cotton Candy

World's Best
Judge

Most People Hula-Hooping
at One Time

World's Smallest Penguins
(found in Chile and New Zealand)

World's Tallest Tree House

World's Longest Sock

World's Loudest Band

World's Biggest Bubble

World's Smallest Pizza

Ah, yes, the World's Longest Sock. This is quite the remarkable story about two people who simply would not give up.

It all started with Nana Nina, who loved knitting. She made socks for her children and her children's children.

She made so many socks, she opened up her own sock shop.

To bring in more customers, she hung a sock outside her door. One long sock.

She added a row after each sale. As the business grew, so did the sock. More and more people came by to see the sock grow. And more people meant more sales.

Nana Nina told people,

"COME SEE THE WORLD'S LONGEST SOCK! I'M GOING TO SET A WORLD RECORD!"

She knew that would make her sock business boom. She invited me, the world records judge, to come see her sock and make it official.

But far away in a forested valley, a lonely lumberman named Chuck was working on another sock that was also super long.

He'd learned to knit on cold, lonely
nights while he watched TV.

He started knitting his sock in episode 1 of *Zombies from New Zealand*
and forgot to stop! By episode 10, his knee-high sock was neck-high!

Then one night, tucked in and ready to snooze,
Chuck sat up when he heard the news.

Today in Chile, Nana Nina set a record for the World's Longest Sock! Crowds are cheering, and everyone has come from miles around to see this incredible sock.

"PEOPLE ARE EXCITED ABOUT THAT SOCK? HECK, MINE IS BETTER!" said Chuck.

"Mine could win the world record. Then I'll be famous! Then I'll have friends!" He picked up his phone and called.

Soon after, Nina was cheerfully chatting with all her new customers when her award was yanked off the wall by yours truly.

On the other side of the world, the usually quiet
valley erupted with noise and excitement. Chuck had
won! Neighbors gathered to celebrate—neighbors
he never even knew he had!

It felt good to have someone
laugh at his jokes.

Someone to talk to
about zombie movies.

Someone to share soup with.

SHEAR

CARD

But Nina would not give up that easily! She pushed up her sleeves and got back to work.

DYE

SPIN

"SORRY, FOLKS,
THIS AWARD HAS
BEEN REVOKED!

Until there is a clear winner, it
will remain unclaimed. These
two socks are too close in size!"

Chuck's neighbors unraveled.

From that point on, NINA AND CHUCK were locked in a fierce competition,

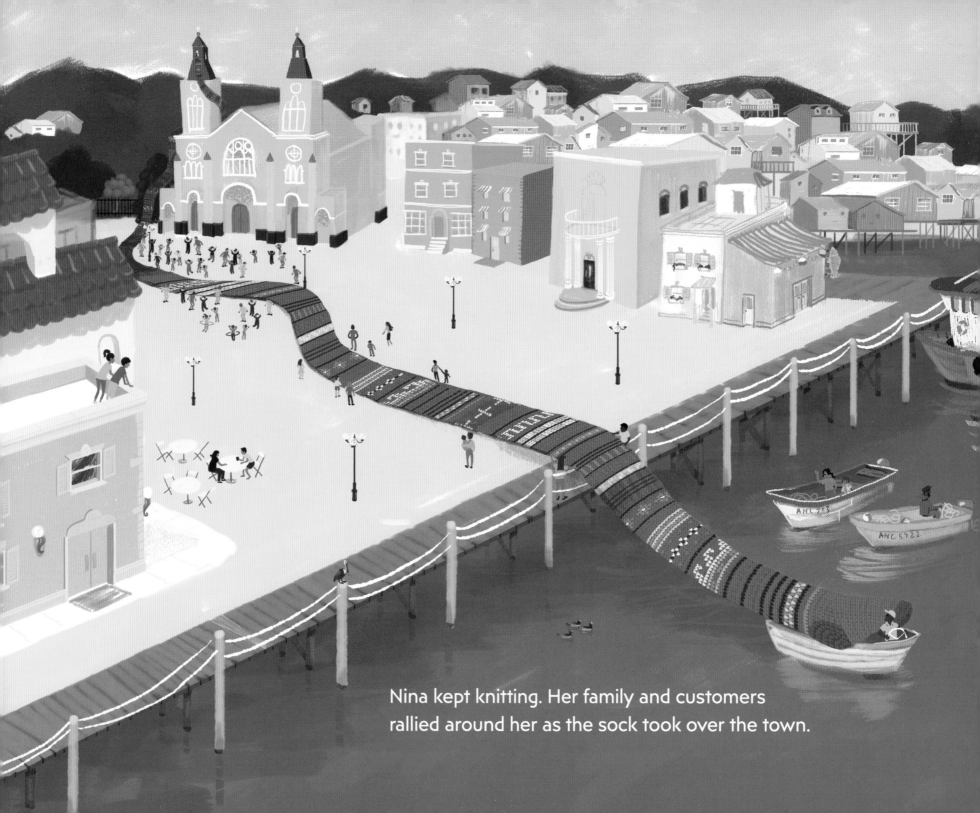

Nina kept knitting. Her family and customers
rallied around her as the sock took over the town.

Time kept ticking, and Chuck kept knitting. His neighbors came to help and cheer him on.

CHUCK! AHEAD BY A FOOT!

THIS IS A REAL NAIL BITER!

WHO WILL WIN THE GREAT SOCK RACE?

Chuck and Nina kept at it.
This competition was

**OUT OF
CONTROL.**

The world was divided.
People took sides.

Nina knitted until her hands were blistered and sore.

Chuck's fingers were numb, and his eyes were blurry. And what was it all for?

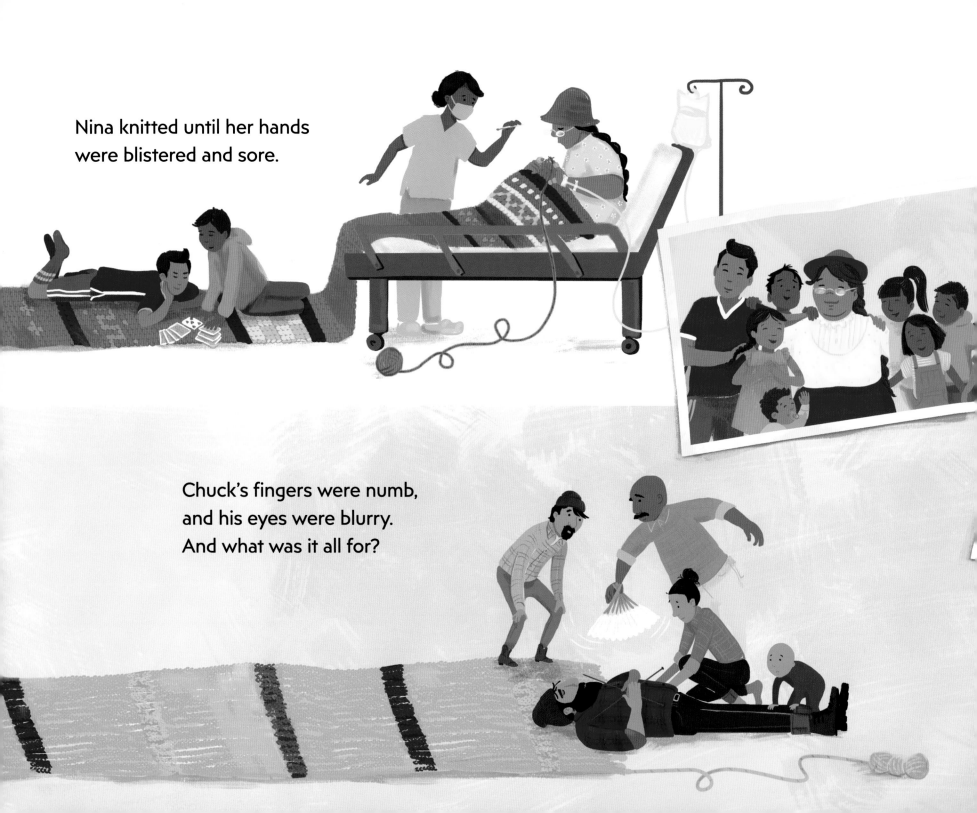

Nina's shop was a success, and her family was proud. But how could she work in her store with her hands like this?

Chuck had found friendship and love—isn't that what he'd really wanted? He'd become a dad. Wasn't that the best reward?

Just when he thought he should stop, a familiar face came on the news . . .

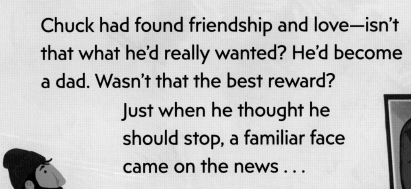

HOUSTON, WE HAVE A SOLUTION!

Together these woolen wonders make

THE WORLD'S LONGEST PAIR OF SOCKS.